MUPPET KIDS IN

New Kid in the Neighborhood

By Ellen Weiss

Illustrated by Tom Cooke

Muppet Press

This 1989 Muppet Press book is published by Longmeadow Press.

Printed in U.S.A.
h g f e d c b a

It was midnight. Every house on Piggy's block was dark and quiet.

Except for the last house on the block, that is. That was the house that had been standing empty for two months, ever since Mr. Evergreen the carpenter had moved away.

But tonight, every window in the big, old house blazed with light. People moved around in all the rooms, and a giant moving van stood outside.

By nine o'clock in the morning, the news was everywhere. There was a new family on the block!

It was a big family, too. Lots of teenage boys...and one girl.

The girl was the best part of all. She was *exactly* Piggy's age.

Piggy jumped out of bed at nine, and by eleven she was all dressed. Lucky for her it was Saturday. There was so much to be done.

The first thing she did was to call Skeeter on the phone. "Did you hear the incredible news?" she asked breathlessly. "There's another girl on the block!"

"I know," said Skeeter. "I went over to visit her already."

This wasn't quite the way Piggy had pictured things. Since she and Skeeter were the only other girls on the block, Piggy had kind of thought they'd go over to the new girl's house together. Or maybe that Piggy would go over there first.

"Well, what's her name? What's she like?" Piggy wanted to know.

"Her name is Janice, and she's really nice. She's very different and interesting."

Hmmmm, thought Piggy. *More different and interesting than me?*

Piggy decided to walk over to Janice's house and see for herself. Carrying some cookies that her mother had baked, she knocked on the door. She waited a minute, and then she knocked harder. At last Janice opened the door, smiling. "I hope you haven't been here too long," she said. "I was playing my guitar." She was wearing a wonderful shirt, and she had a nice face.

Janice thanked Piggy for the cookies and put them down on the hall table next to a huge plate of brownies, which were wrapped up with a pretty bow. FROM YOUR NEW NEIGHBOR, SKEETER, said the card.

Later that afternoon, Piggy and Skeeter took Janice on a tour of the neighborhood.

"Would you like to see the firehouse?" asked Skeeter.

"For sure," said Janice. It sounded neat when she said it.

"Hi, girls," said one of the fire fighters. "Would you like to climb up and sit in the fire truck?"

"Thank you very much, but I think it might be a little dirty, don't you agree?" said Piggy, turning to her friends.

"No way! Here I come!" said Skeeter, heading for the truck.

"For sure!" agreed Janice.

Piggy watched them beep the horn.

9127

"That was fun," said Skeeter.

"Really," said Janice.

"What shall we do now?" asked Piggy. "Would you like to go to the ice-cream parlor for a teensy something?"

"Actually," said Skeeter, "I'd like to go to the music store, if you don't mind. I need some new drumsticks."

"You play the drums?" said Janice. "That's great! We can play together!"

Piggy was beginning to feel very left out.

In the music store, the three girls looked at records.
"Ooh," sighed Piggy. "A Johnny Smoothness album. He's so dreamy."
"Hey, look at this," said Janice. "Rollo and the Wreckers. My brother gave me one of their albums. They're so cool."
"Looks great," said Skeeter.
"Do you want to come over to my house and listen to it?" said Janice.
"Sure!" said Skeeter.
"You can come, too," Janice said to Piggy.

At Janice's house, they all ate cookies and drank mint tea.

"Your house is sure different from any house I've ever been in," said Skeeter.

"I'll say," said Piggy. It was a strange place, but she liked it.

Sunday was bright and sunny. Piggy got out of bed at noon and called Skeeter's number right away. She thought that the two of them could go over to Janice's and show her some more of the neighborhood.

Skeeter didn't answer, so Piggy picked out some purple socks and headed over to Janice's by herself. It would be nice to be alone with Janice, anyway, she thought.

Halfway there, Piggy ran into Skeeter and Janice.

"I just called you," she said to Skeeter.

"Oh, Skeeter and I have been riding around for two hours," said Janice. "Want to join us?" Piggy just sighed.

They rode around the neighborhood, and Skeeter slowed down and pointed when they passed the park. "The playground here is really nice. It has a tree house," she said.

"A tree house!" cried Janice. "I had one where I used to live." She looked sad.

"I'll take you over there tomorrow after school, when there's more time," said Skeeter. "You'll feel better, you'll see."

Now it was Piggy who looked sad. "I have my ballet lesson tomorrow afternoon," she said. "I guess I can't go."

"Don't worry, there'll be lots of other times," said Skeeter.

Suddenly, Janice's bike made a clanking noise. She looked down. "Oh, rats," she said. "The chain came off."

"Oh, I can fix that," said Skeeter. She took some tools out of her bike pack, bent down, and had the chain back on in a minute.

"You are great," said Janice in admiration.

They rode on, and in a few blocks they passed the bakery. The windows were full of wonderful things to eat.

"I happen to have my entire allowance with me," said Piggy. "Should we go in and buy something?"

"I can't. I spent my whole allowance on comic books," said Skeeter.

"And I spent mine on guitar strings," said Janice. "Let's go check out the school."

"So, this is it," said Janice.

"Yep, this is it," said Skeeter.

"I'm a little nervous about my first day," said Janice.

"When you get to school tomorrow, I'll show you where to hang your book bag and everything," said Piggy.

"I have an idea," said Skeeter. "Why don't I pick you up on the way to school? Then I can show you where to go in."

"That would be great," said Janice.

On the way home, they bumped into Rowlf, who was delivering newspapers.

"Rowlf, this is Janice," called Skeeter, as Rowlf sped by. "She's our new friend."

"Pleased to meet you, Janice," shouted Rowlf.

As the sun began to set, Piggy and Skeeter finally dropped Janice off at her house. Then they walked their bikes slowly toward Piggy's.

"So, I guess I'll see you tomorrow morning," said Skeeter.

"A lot you care," said Piggy under her breath.

"Aren't you going to pick up Janice with me?" said Skeeter.

"I wasn't invited," sniffed Piggy.

"Well, I certainly *meant* for you to come," explained Skeeter.

"Sure, sure," said Piggy.

"Piggy, what's wrong?"

"Nothing. Nothing at all," sniffed Piggy even louder.

"There *is* something wrong," said Skeeter. "Tell me."

"I don't want to talk about it," snuffled Piggy.

"Okay," said Skeeter with a shrug.

"All right, I'll tell you," said Piggy. "Ever since Janice came to town, I feel like you're—like you're not my friend anymore. I'm just someone who hangs around. Someone who tags along with you and Janice."

"I get it," said Skeeter. "You're jealous."

"No, I'm not! Well, maybe I am," said Piggy miserably. "Maybe I am j-j-j..." Piggy could not even say the word, it was so awful and embarrassing.

"You're just being silly, Piggy," said Skeeter.

"No, I'm not, Skeeter," said Piggy. "You've been acting like you hardly know me."

Skeeter thought about it. Then she gave Piggy a big hug. "I guess I have, a little," she said.

"A lot," said Piggy.

"A lot," agreed Skeeter. "And I'm sorry. You're very important to me, and I would never want to hurt your feelings."

The next day, Piggy and Skeeter picked up Janice and they all walked to school together.

On the way, it started to rain.

"Would you both like to come under my umbrella?" asked Piggy. "I think we can all fit."

"Thanks, Piggy!" said Janice and Skeeter.

They ran into school just as the bell was ringing and waited for Janice, who went into the office to find out who her teacher would be.

"Oh, you have Mr. Bumper," said Skeeter when Janice came out. "He's really nice. And you'll be in Kermit's class."

"You're so lucky!" said Piggy.

After school, they all met at the front door.

"How was your first day?" Piggy asked breathlessly.

"It was fun," said Janice. "I'm going to like it a lot. Can we go to the tree house now?"

"Why don't we wait till tomorrow, when Piggy can come, too?" suggested Skeeter.

"For sure," said Janice.

They walked home. The rain had stopped and the sun was shining again.

"This is a really great neighborhood," said Janice happily.

"And it's full of really good friends," added Piggy.